My Treasury of
Scary Stories

My Treasury of
Scary Stories

Written by
Caroline Repchuk, Claire Keene,
Geoff Cowan, Kat Wootton, and Candy Wallace

Illustrated by
Diana Catchpole, Robin Edmunds,
Chris Forsey, and Claire Mumford

Cover illustrated by
Steve Boulter

Bath · New York · Singapore · Hong Kong · Cologne · Delhi · Melbourne

This editon published by Parragon in 2007

Parragon
Queen Street House
4 Queen Street
Bath BA1 1HE, UK

Copyright © Parragon Books Ltd 1999

ISBN: 978-1-4054-9871-5

Printed in China

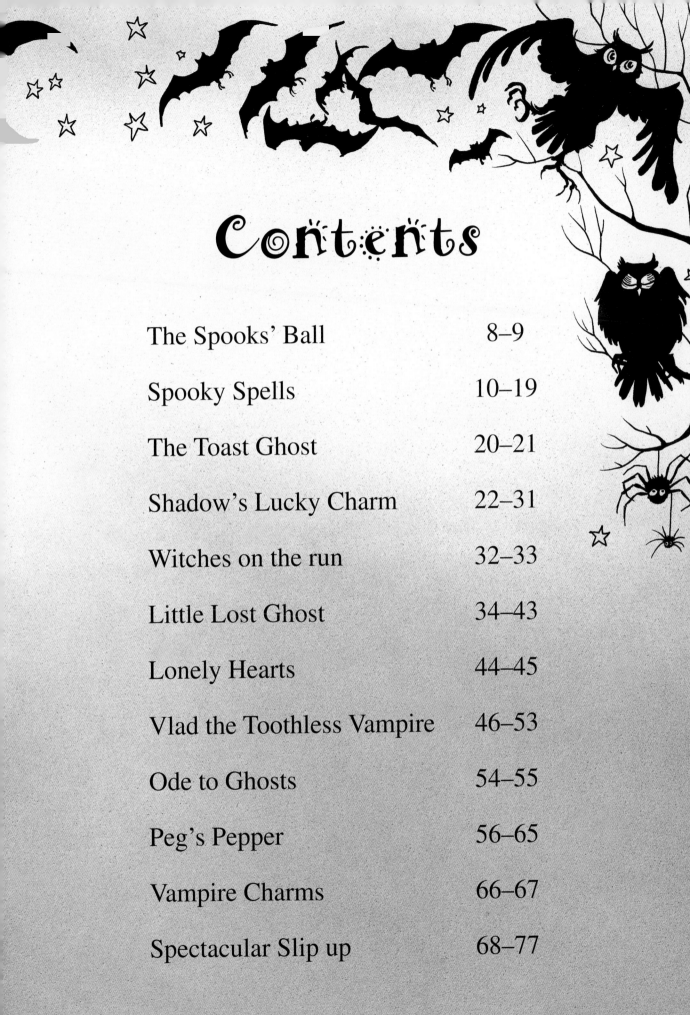

Contents

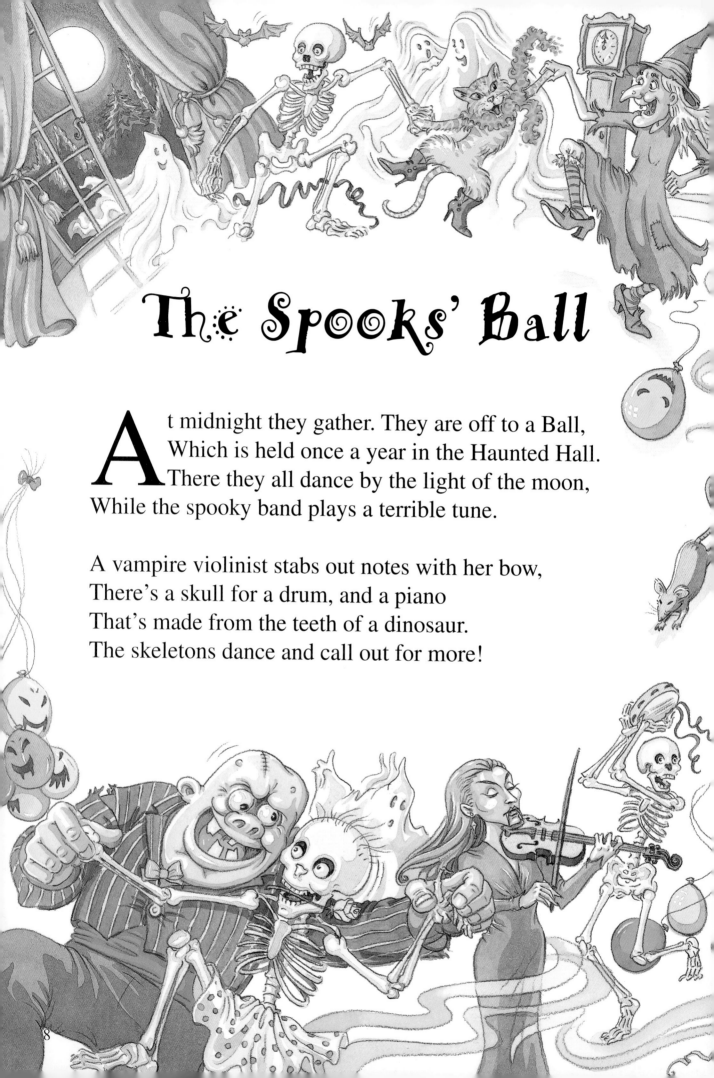

The Spooks' Ball

At midnight they gather. They are off to a Ball,
Which is held once a year in the Haunted Hall.
There they all dance by the light of the moon,
While the spooky band plays a terrible tune.

A vampire violinist stabs out notes with her bow,
There's a skull for a drum, and a piano
That's made from the teeth of a dinosaur.
The skeletons dance and call out for more!

There's a ghost with his head tucked under his arm.
He feeds it with potato chips without causing alarm.
A witch and her cat are dancing a jig.
But the witch can't keep up 'cos her boots are too big.

But the time will soon come for the sun to rise,
And the spooks will all vanish before your eyes.
They've had such frightful fun at the Ball tonight,
Will you see them next year? Well you just might…

9

Spooky Spells

"It's almost Halloween again," said Snitchy Witch to her black cat Treacle. "I must make the food for the Witches' Convention." She sat down to write her shopping list: 2 newts; 3 frogs; bag of snails; can of slug juice; 1 rat's tail; package of mixed spiders… She didn't notice the little ghost watching from behind the cauldron…

Now, this Halloween was extra special for Snitchy Witch. She was hosting the Witches' Halloween Convention in the ballroom of the Haunted House, hired specially for the occasion. Witches were coming from far and wide to attend lectures on topics such as *Magic Brooms and How to Handle Them; Growing Warts in a Week,* and *If You Want to Get Ahead, Get a Cat!*

The highlight would be a Spelling Contest, where the witches would compete for the title of Witch of the Year.

"Just wait until it's my turn," said Snitchy Witch as she finished her list. "I'll show 'em a thing or two!" and she hurried off on her broomstick to the store.

As soon as she had gone, Spooky, the ghost, came out from behind the cauldron.

He didn't like stinky witches, and he had no intention of putting up with a whole houseful of them. Having just one in the Haunted House was bad enough—but a whole convention! It was no use trying to frighten them away. Withces weren't afraid of a little ghost like him. But perhaps there was a way to make them scare themselves... Spooky smiled. He would have some fun with those silly old witches…

Snitchy Witch returned and spent the rest of the day cooking up the most disgusting food she could think of. Then she dusted off her spell book and polished her magic wand. She could hardly wait to demonstrate her "garden slug into gooey chocolate cake" spell! From behind the cauldron, Spooky watched her every move...

13

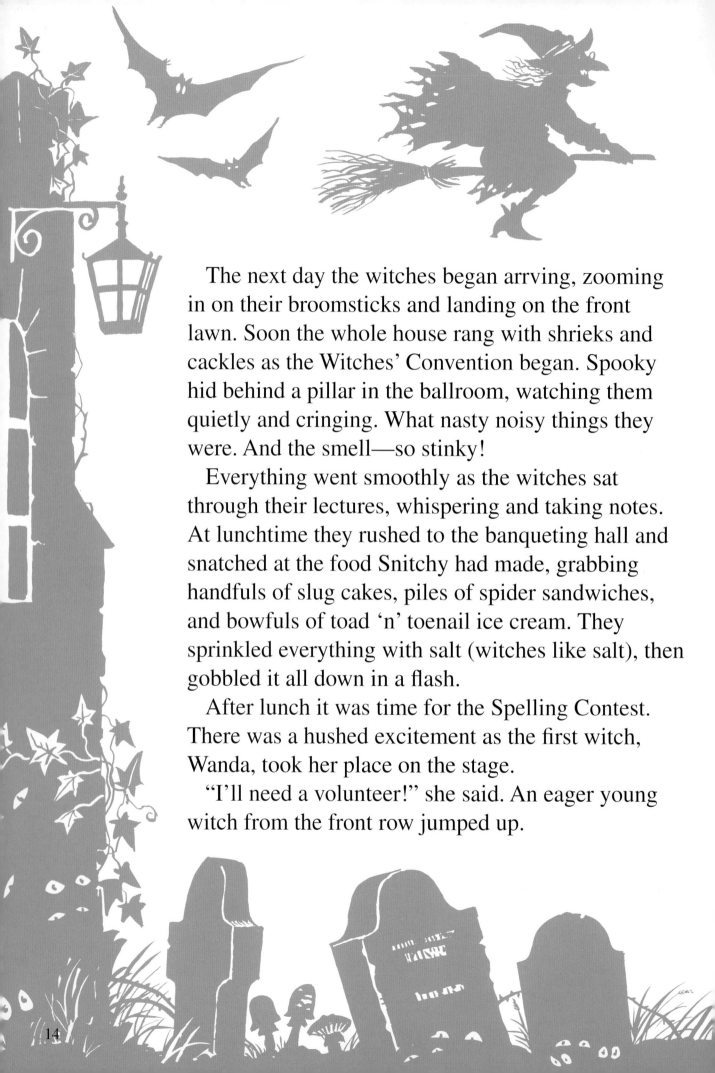

The next day the witches began arrving, zooming in on their broomsticks and landing on the front lawn. Soon the whole house rang with shrieks and cackles as the Witches' Convention began. Spooky hid behind a pillar in the ballroom, watching them quietly and cringing. What nasty noisy things they were. And the smell—so stinky!

Everything went smoothly as the witches sat through their lectures, whispering and taking notes. At lunchtime they rushed to the banqueting hall and snatched at the food Snitchy had made, grabbing handfuls of slug cakes, piles of spider sandwiches, and bowfuls of toad 'n' toenail ice cream. They sprinkled everything with salt (witches like salt), then gobbled it all down in a flash.

After lunch it was time for the Spelling Contest. There was a hushed excitement as the first witch, Wanda, took her place on the stage.

"I'll need a volunteer!" she said. An eager young witch from the front row jumped up.

15

"You're in for a treat!" said Wanda. "I'm going to turn you into a stinking sewer rat! Just temporarily, of course."

"Ooh, lovely," said the volunteer. "What fun."

Wanda raised her arms, waved her magic wand, and muttered the magic spell:

"She's not the last, she'll be the first, come mystic magic, do your worst!"

The witches watched with eager anticipation, as with a loud bang, a great flash, and a crackle of sparks the volunteer witch transformed before their eyes. But what was this? Instead of becoming a stinking rat, she had changed into a beautiful princess! Wanda looked at her in

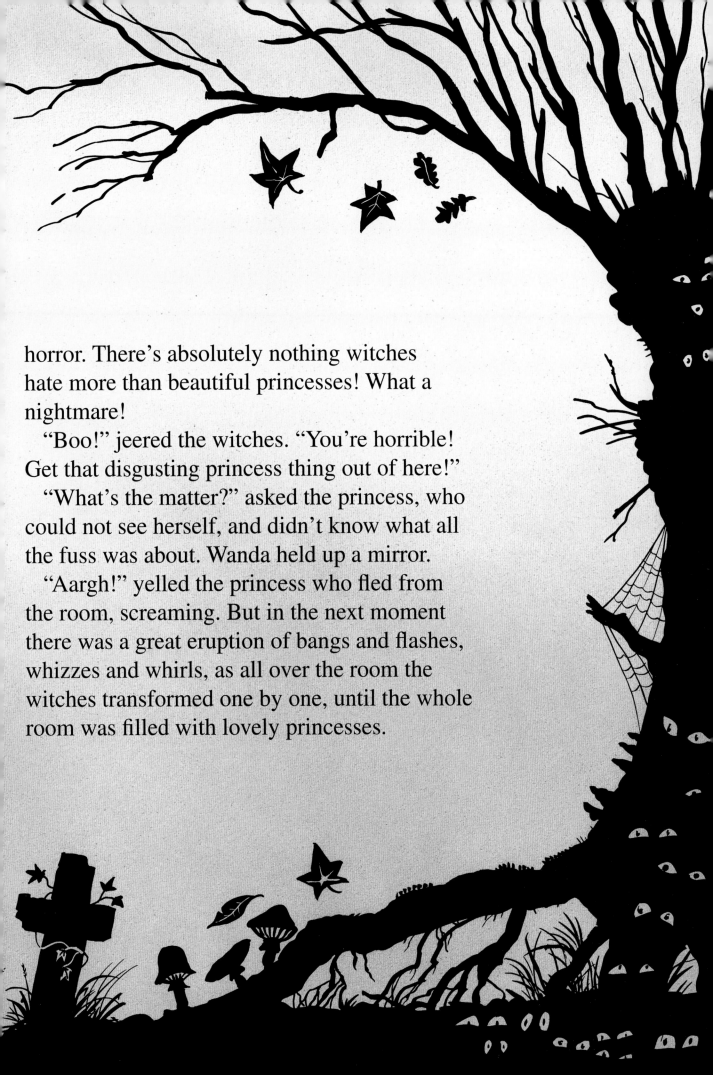

horror. There's absolutely nothing witches
hate more than beautiful princesses! What a
nightmare!

"Boo!" jeered the witches. "You're horrible!
Get that disgusting princess thing out of here!"

"What's the matter?" asked the princess, who
could not see herself, and didn't know what all
the fuss was about. Wanda held up a mirror.

"Aargh!" yelled the princess who fled from
the room, screaming. But in the next moment
there was a great eruption of bangs and flashes,
whizzes and whirls, as all over the room the
witches transformed one by one, until the whole
room was filled with lovely princesses.

Then, what a fuss and commotion! They hollered and screamed, clutching at their shiny hair and beautiful gowns. Spooky laughed until he cried, for of course the commotion was all his fault. He had made a spell for princesses which he found at the back of Snitchy Witch's spell book while she was out shopping. "Only to be used on your worst enemies, or in emergencies" it had said. Spooky decided this was definitely an emergency, and had added the spell to the salt (which, as you remember, the witches had used plenty of on their lunch!).

Still yelling and screaming, the princesses leaped on their brooms and fled.

"Come back!" yelled Snitchy Witch (now a princess herself). "We haven't finished the contest!" But it was no use. The witches, or rather princesses, had gone. Spooky stretched out on an old couch and grinned. Peace and quiet once more. Only one stinky witch left in the Haunted House, and even she wasn't too bad now she was a princess!

The Toast Ghost

A hungry ghost wished for some toast,
"I'd eat a loaf!" he'd often boast.
The words he longed someone to utter,
Were "Here's hot toast with lots of butter!"

The ghost lived in a ruined house.
He shared it with a little mouse.
It squeaked, "No toast! Don't even look!
There is no toaster, nor a cook!"

The ghost despaired, "What shall I do?"
The mouse replied, "If I were you,
I'd seek a café or a restaurant,
Ask them to make the toast you want!"

The ghost soon found the perfect spot.
He dreamed of toast, lovely and hot.
He waited for the cafe to close,
While smells all toasty teased his nose.

He went inside and found the kitchen.
For buttered toast the ghost was itchin'!
Then something white behind the door,
Floated softly to the floor.

The nervous ghost took off in fright—
He found he'd lost his appetite.
"That's really put me off my treat!"
But let me tell, 'tween you and me—
It was the chef's white hat he saw.
That ghost, he don't eat toast no more!

Shadow's Lucky Charm

Dark shadows of evening hung over the television studios. Bustling by day, with actors and cameramen, makeup experts and producers, now everyone had gone home and the place stood empty. Only Sam, the security officer, remained. His flashlight shone upon doors and windows as he made his rounds, checking everything was shut down safely until morning.

23

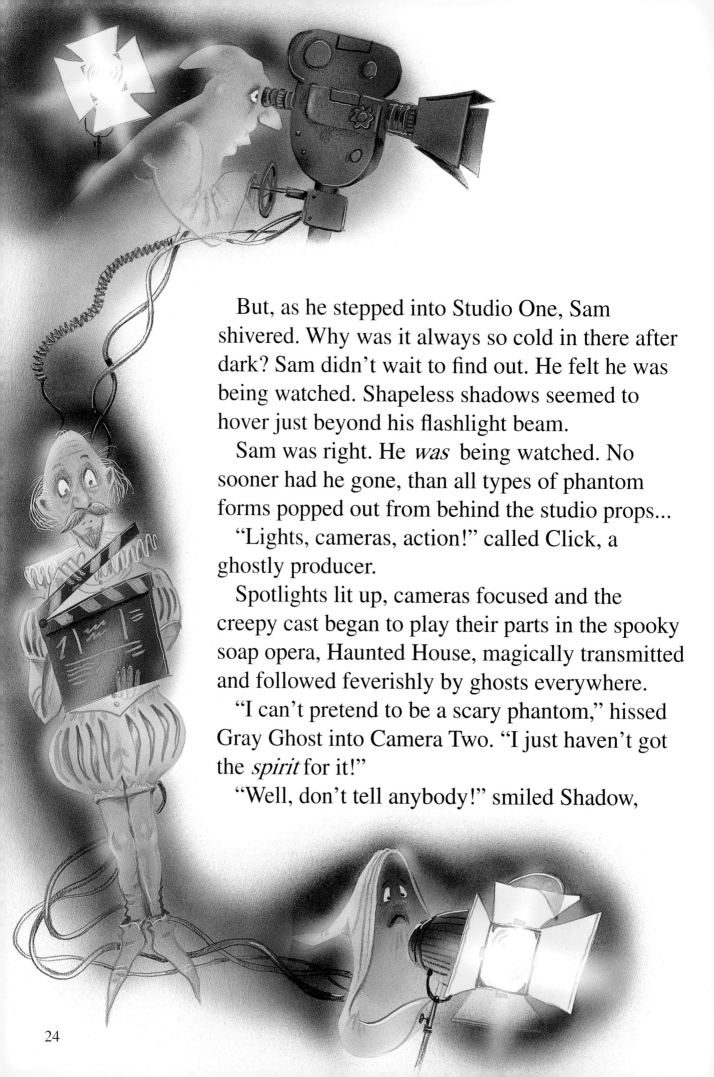

But, as he stepped into Studio One, Sam shivered. Why was it always so cold in there after dark? Sam didn't wait to find out. He felt he was being watched. Shapeless shadows seemed to hover just beyond his flashlight beam.

Sam was right. He *was* being watched. No sooner had he gone, than all types of phantom forms popped out from behind the studio props...

"Lights, cameras, action!" called Click, a ghostly producer.

Spotlights lit up, cameras focused and the creepy cast began to play their parts in the spooky soap opera, Haunted House, magically transmitted and followed feverishly by ghosts everywhere.

"I can't pretend to be a scary phantom," hissed Gray Ghost into Camera Two. "I just haven't got the *spirit* for it!"

"Well, don't tell anybody!" smiled Shadow,

delivering her lines in the lead role. "It'll be our secret. Besides..."

Suddenly, she froze. There was an awkward silence as the others looked around in confusion and waited for her to go on. Surely she hadn't forgotten her lines? After what seemed like an age she continued: "...I've enough ghostly groans for the two of us! I'll show you."

Star of the series, Shadow carried on as if nothing had happened. Her grimaces were so ghastly, the rest of the cast would have been scared to death, if they were alive.

Meanwhile, in every haunted home across the country, a ghostly audience tuned in to the supernatural series. While humans slept, countless television screens came to life. But only specters could see the phantom pictures.

Back at the studios, another episode ended.

"Cut! Another out-of-this-world performance, Shadow!" said Click. "You're the star of the show! But you had us worried there for a spell."

The other spooks gathered around. Shadow looked even more deathly white than usual.

"What's wrong?" asked Gray Ghost, gliding toward her like swirling smoke. "You froze—that's not like you!"

"I'm afraid I can't go on any more. I'm going to have to leave the show," said Shadow, unhappily.

The studio echoed eerily with shocked gasps.

"You, leave? Impossible!" cried Click. "Name whatever you want to stay and it's yours!"

"I'm sorry but there's nothing you can give me," said Shadow. "I've lost my lucky wishbone. I've always kept it near me while I'm acting. I can't go on without it—I get terrible stage fright. The studio cleaners must have swept it up and thrown it away."

Click gently touched Shadow's frosty cheek with a crooked, bony finger.

"You've been working too hard," he smiled. "A party will cheer you up!"

So the next night, as soon as the cameras stopped rolling, they threw a party for Shadow. The creepy cast did all they could to make her feel better. Two ghosts slipped into a costume horse from the wardrobe department and galloped through the air. A spectral blob called Slimy slithered around, changing shape. He dripped down the walls and spread like shiny, green goo across the floor. Knuckles, a skeleton, pretended to step on him and slip. The ghosts wailed with

laughter, all except Shadow. She kept glancing at the cameras and worrying about her lost lucky charm.

Next moment, the sweetest black cat Shadow had ever seen stepped through the wall of the studio. As it trotted over to her, Shadow could see right through its little body. She was enchanted, and reached out her hand to stroke it.

"Who are you?" asked Shadow.

"I'm Lucky," purred the cat. "I move as silently as a shadow."

"Shadow is my name!" laughed Shadow.

"Can I look around? I've always wanted to be in a TV show," mewed Lucky.

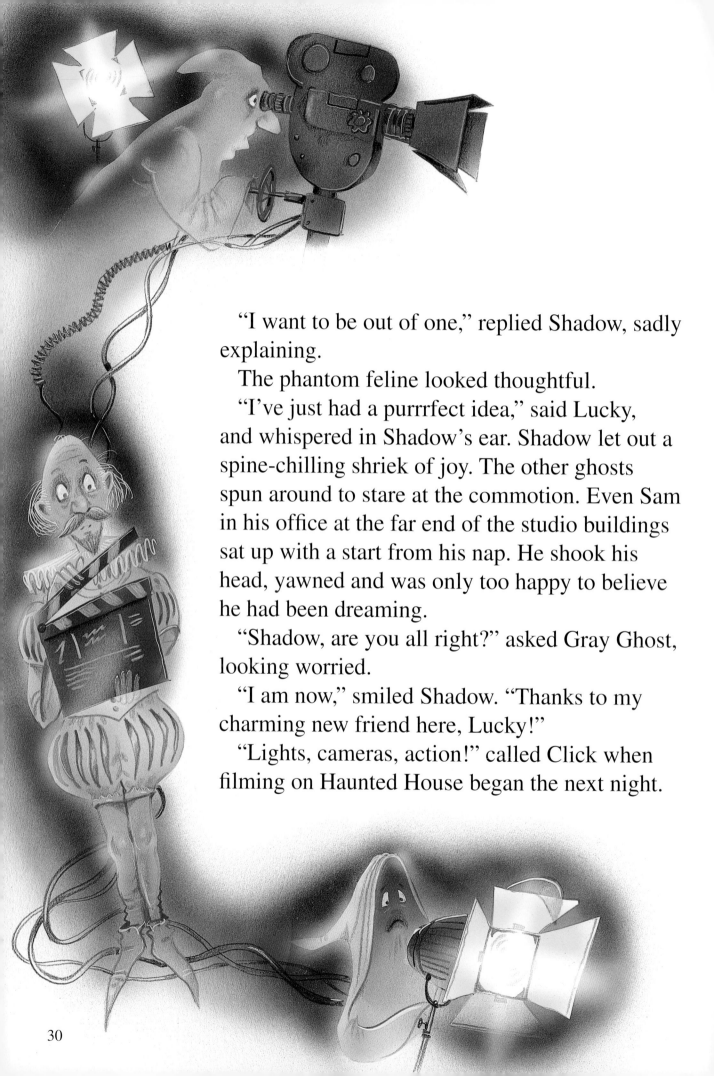

"I want to be out of one," replied Shadow, sadly explaining.

The phantom feline looked thoughtful.

"I've just had a purrrfect idea," said Lucky, and whispered in Shadow's ear. Shadow let out a spine-chilling shriek of joy. The other ghosts spun around to stare at the commotion. Even Sam in his office at the far end of the studio buildings sat up with a start from his nap. He shook his head, yawned and was only too happy to believe he had been dreaming.

"Shadow, are you all right?" asked Gray Ghost, looking worried.

"I am now," smiled Shadow. "Thanks to my charming new friend here, Lucky!"

"Lights, cameras, action!" called Click when filming on Haunted House began the next night.

This time joining the high-spirited cast, there was an extra ghost. Lucky was delighted to have been given a glide-on part. Shadow was even happier about it. Her faultless performance proved it. After all, Shadow had a new lucky charm. And as for any stage fright, there simply wasn't a ghost of a chance it would return now!

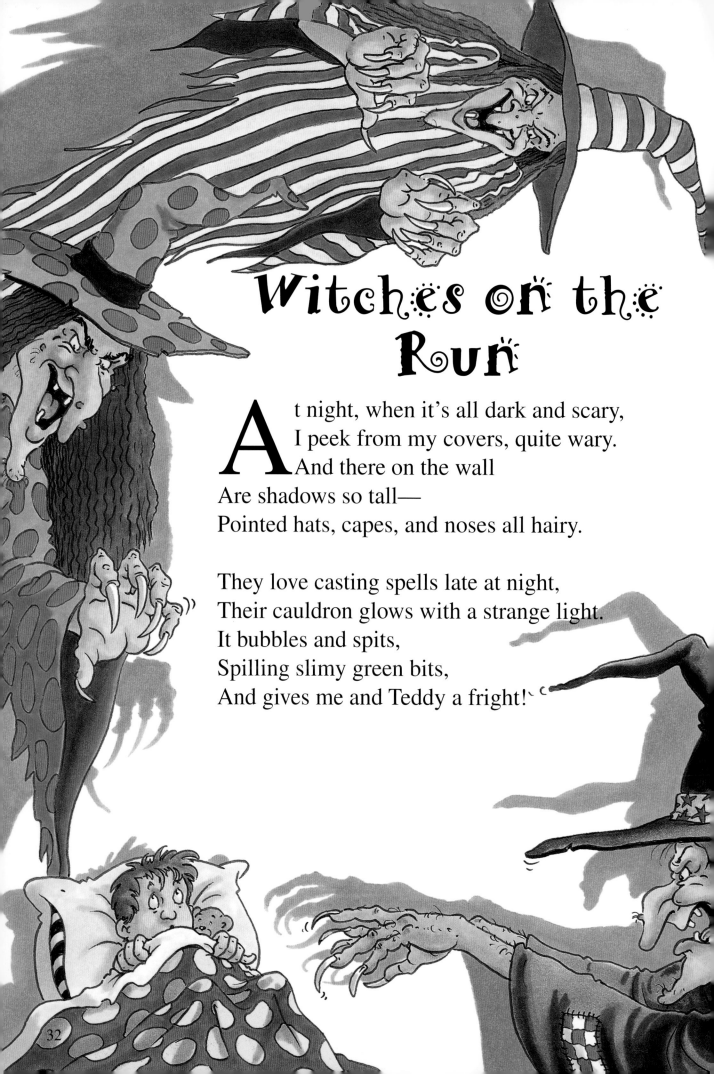

Witches on the Run

At night, when it's all dark and scary,
I peek from my covers, quite wary.
And there on the wall
Are shadows so tall—
Pointed hats, capes, and noses all hairy.

They love casting spells late at night,
Their cauldron glows with a strange light.
It bubbles and spits,
Spilling slimy green bits,
And gives me and Teddy a fright!

My mom says that I must be dreaming,
When I spy witches high on the ceiling.
But they keep me awake
With the noise that they make,
All that ear-piercing cackling and screaming!

But tonight when they come I'll be ready,
All I need is to keep my aim steady.
One squirt from my gun,
Will have them on the run,
Witches hate getting wet—don't they Teddy?

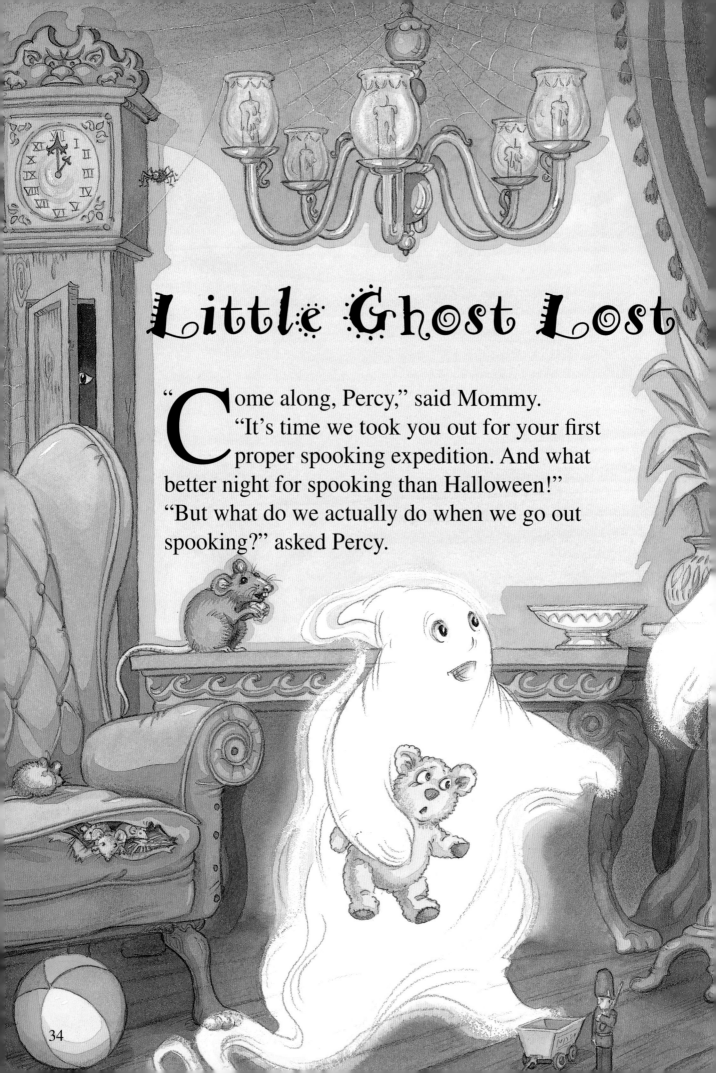

Little Ghost Lost

"Come along, Percy," said Mommy. "It's time we took you out for your first proper spooking expedition. And what better night for spooking than Halloween!"

"But what do we actually do when we go out spooking?" asked Percy.

"Just follow us and copy what we do and you'll soon find out," said Daddy. "But you must remember to stick close, and don't wander off on your own."

With that, Mr. and Mrs. Ghost and their young son Percy set off on their first night of spooking together. They floated up the chimney of their home in the Haunted House, and curled out of the top like whisps of smoke. They hovered over the rooftop, then slunk off into the cover of night.

"I don't like it out here," said Percy, timidly. "It's too dark!"

"Don't be silly," said Mommy. "Ghosts aren't afraid of the dark!"

At the edge of some woods they came to a cottage, with a fire glowing dimly inside.

An old man was heading down the path toward the woodpile.

"Follow me," said Daddy. "This will be fun!"

The ghosts hid and watched as the old man piled logs high in his arms. Then with a terrible wail Mr. and Mrs. Ghost rose up from behind the woodpile and the old man leaped in the air in fright, sending the wood flying. He ran back to his cottage hollering and screaming, and the ghosts collapsed in giggles.

"That was cool!" said Percy.

Next they came to a house with a pumpkin in the window. Peering in, they saw a woman baking pumpkin pie. She turned to see three ghostly faces pressed against

the glass. She threw her arms up, screaming, knocked over a bag of flour, and smothered herself from head to toe.

"She looks pretty ghostly herself, now!" laughed Percy.

All through the evening the family of ghosts played ghostly pranks, jumping out and spooking folk, and squealing with delight as they ran away, screaming. Percy grew braver and bolder each time, copying his parents' ghastly expressions and gruesome groans.

"I'm a natural at this," thought Percy, smugly. "I bet I could spook someone all on my own!"

So as soon as his mommy and daddy turned their backs, the naughty little ghost hurried after two children he had spotted up ahead. Creeping up behind them, he set his face in its most fearsome expression, got ready to give his most spooky wail, then tapped them on their shoulders. But, as the children spun around, Percy froze in horror. Instead of the two sweet-faced children he had expected

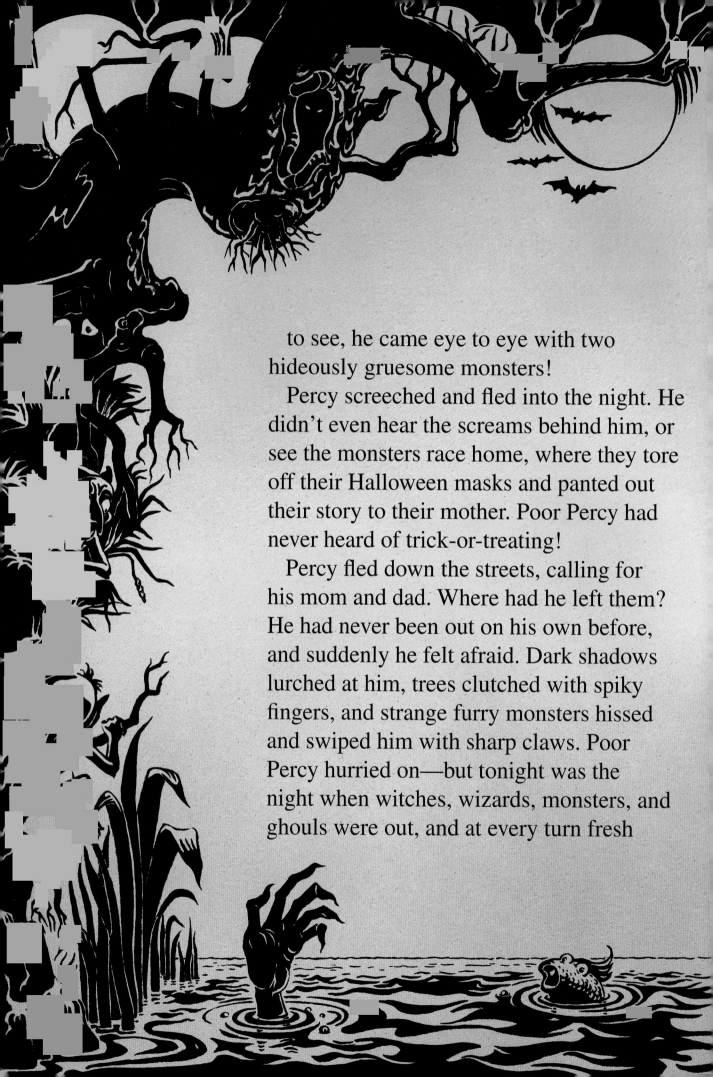

to see, he came eye to eye with two hideously gruesome monsters!

Percy screeched and fled into the night. He didn't even hear the screams behind him, or see the monsters race home, where they tore off their Halloween masks and panted out their story to their mother. Poor Percy had never heard of trick-or-treating!

Percy fled down the streets, calling for his mom and dad. Where had he left them? He had never been out on his own before, and suddenly he felt afraid. Dark shadows lurched at him, trees clutched with spiky fingers, and strange furry monsters hissed and swiped him with sharp claws. Poor Percy hurried on—but tonight was the night when witches, wizards, monsters, and ghouls were out, and at every turn fresh

horrors awaited. Finally he sank exhausted in a doorway.

"I want my mommy!" he wailed, and began to cry. Before long he had cried himself to sleep. Hours later he woke with a start. Something was poking and prodding him with a sharp stick.
"What have we here then?" said a mean little voice.

"Looks like a young ghostie—we can have some fun with him. Let's pinch him!" said another nasty voice. The voices belonged to two goblins—mean, dirty, smelly little goblins, with sharp noses, pointed ears, and bony fingers.

"BOO!" said Percy, pulling his most scary face. "Leave me alone!"

But the goblins just burst out laughing—it takes a lot to frighten goblins.

"Is that the best you can do?" they taunted, poking poor Percy again. He howled and wailed and tried his best to scare them away, but they just laughed and pinched him even harder.

"You can't scare us!" they teased."Nothing scares us!"

"Oh no?" said a deep voice behind them. "How about this!"

The goblins turned to see two huge, terrifying ghosts ready to pounce. "Help!" they cried, fleeing into the night!

"Mommy! Daddy!" cried Percy in delight. "You found me!"

Soon the ghost family were safely back in the Haunted House.

"I'm never going to make a good spook!" said Percy miserably.

"Yes you will," soothed Mommy, tucking him into bed. "After all, you sure scared us! Next time, stick close!"

"I promise," said Percy, and in no time at all he was sound asleep, dreaming of ways to spook goblins.

Lonely Hearts

Fun-loving troll, dirty and smelly,
With damp slimy skin and big hairy belly,
Nice muddy fingers and grubby wet toes,
Hot, steamy breath and rings through each nose.

With stains on his shirt and holes in his socks,
Teeth that need cleaning and knots in his locks,
Tears in his pants and scuffs on his shoe,
He's waiting to meet someone lovely like you.

He likes dirty ditches and hiding in holes,
Is certain to win when he fights other trolls.
Is very attentive, will woo you with roses,
After he's used them to pick both his noses.

He lives on his own, in a dark stinking pit,
Oozing with slime and covered in spit.
Now feeling lonely, he hopes there's a chance
He can meet someone similar for fun and romance!

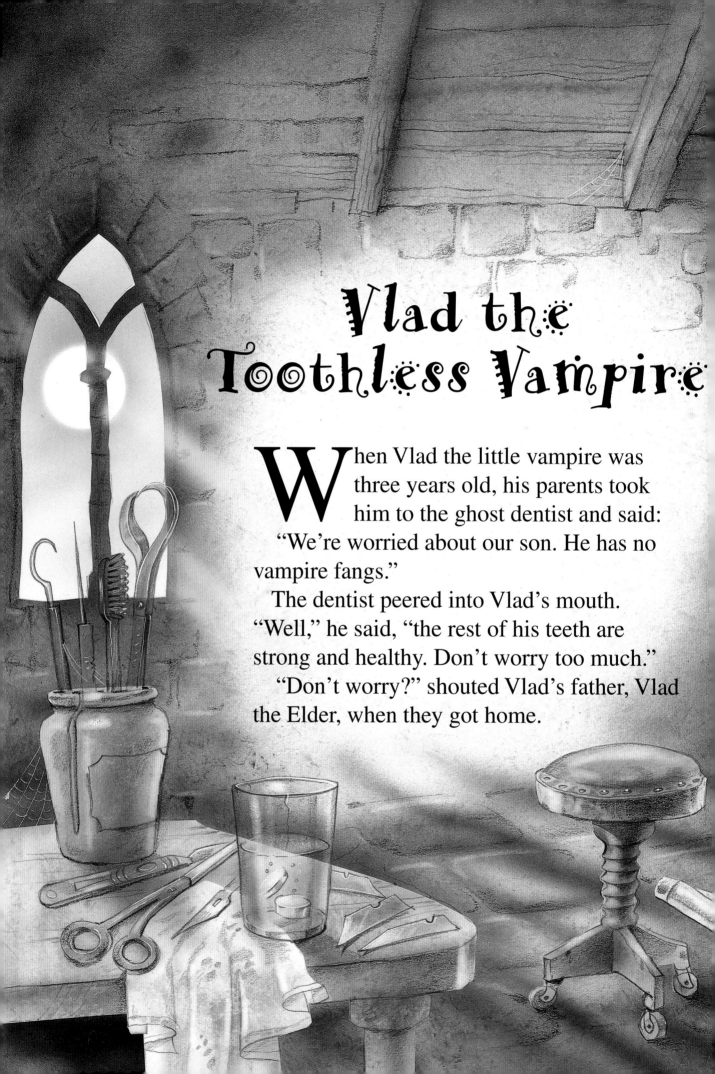

Vlad the Toothless Vampire

When Vlad the little vampire was three years old, his parents took him to the ghost dentist and said:

"We're worried about our son. He has no vampire fangs."

The dentist peered into Vlad's mouth. "Well," he said, "the rest of his teeth are strong and healthy. Don't worry too much."

"Don't worry?" shouted Vlad's father, Vlad the Elder, when they got home.

"How can I not worry? Generations of our family have had perfect razor-sharp fangs!"

"Calm down, dear," said his wife, gently.

"How can I calm down?!" shouted Vlad the Elder.

"Why, I myself won *Most Ferocious Fangs* two years running at the Supernatural Show. He's an embarrassment to the family!"

"He's very good at other things," soothed Vlad's mother Val. "He turns into a very big bat, and he has lovely glossy hair."

"What use is hair when you want to bite someone?" shouted Vlad the Elder. "What's he going to do? TICKLE the blood out of them?!" He was so furious that he changed into a bat and flew off.

By the time Vlad was twelve, he still had no fangs. He wished his father could be proud of him, but

Vlad the Elder always seemed disappointed in him.

"Twelve years old and no vampire teeth!" he raged.

"He'll never make a proper vampire. He's no use at all!"

Young Vlad was hurt and angry: "I don't have to bite things!" he cried. "I could be a doctor, or a vet, or an actor!"

"Pah!" snorted his father. "A vet who only works at night? Don't be a fool, son."

A short time later, a local drama group decided to use the old abandoned house in which Vlad and his family lived as a venue for their next show, *Dracula*.

"It's got a great spooky atmosphere," said Brian the director, unaware the basement housed a family of vampires, one of whom was listening. Vlad was hanging on the lamp shade disguised as a bat.

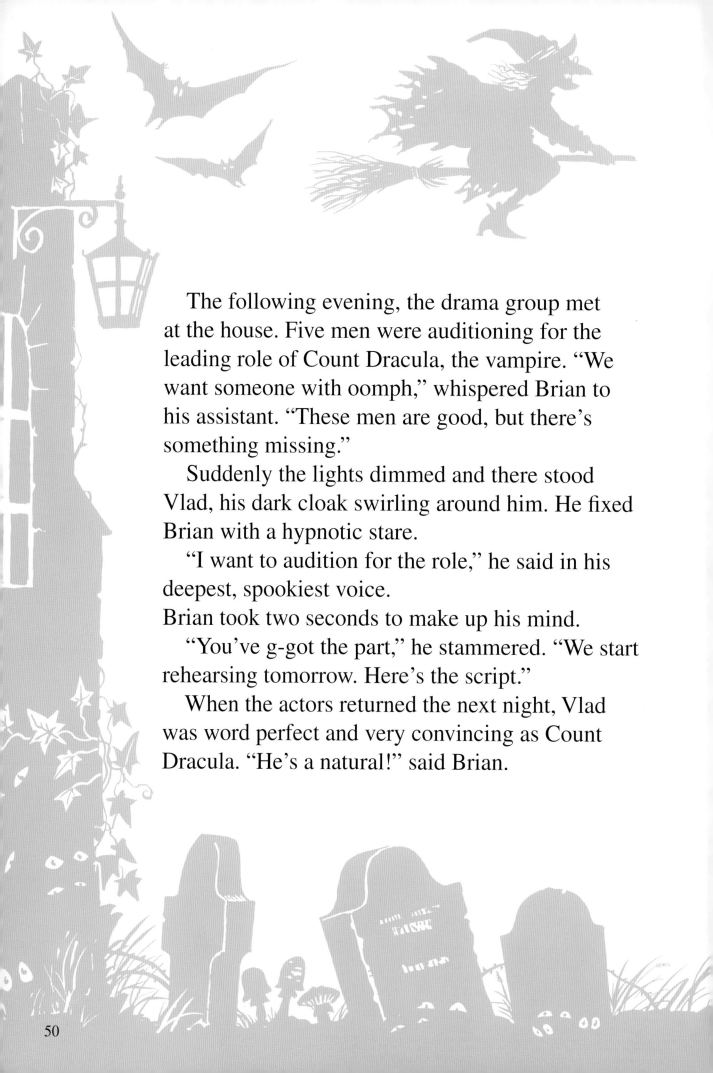

The following evening, the drama group met at the house. Five men were auditioning for the leading role of Count Dracula, the vampire. "We want someone with oomph," whispered Brian to his assistant. "These men are good, but there's something missing."

Suddenly the lights dimmed and there stood Vlad, his dark cloak swirling around him. He fixed Brian with a hypnotic stare.

"I want to audition for the role," he said in his deepest, spookiest voice.
Brian took two seconds to make up his mind.

"You've g-got the part," he stammered. "We start rehearsing tomorrow. Here's the script."

When the actors returned the next night, Vlad was word perfect and very convincing as Count Dracula. "He's a natural!" said Brian.

Two months later, the play was ready, the tickets were sold out and most of the villagers were coming to see the performance.

Vlad had not told his father about his acting, but when it came to the opening night, Vlad's mother said to her husband: "There's something you ought to see upstairs tonight, dear." So, disguised as bats, they hung on the curtains to watch.

Vlad was terrific. The audience clapped and cheered at the end. Someone said:

"You'd think he was a real vampire. I bet his parents are proud of him."

Vlad's father realized how unfair he had been to his son. "I suppose sharp teeth aren't everything," he said to his wife, looking ashamed. He vowed to accept his son for the remarkable boy he was.

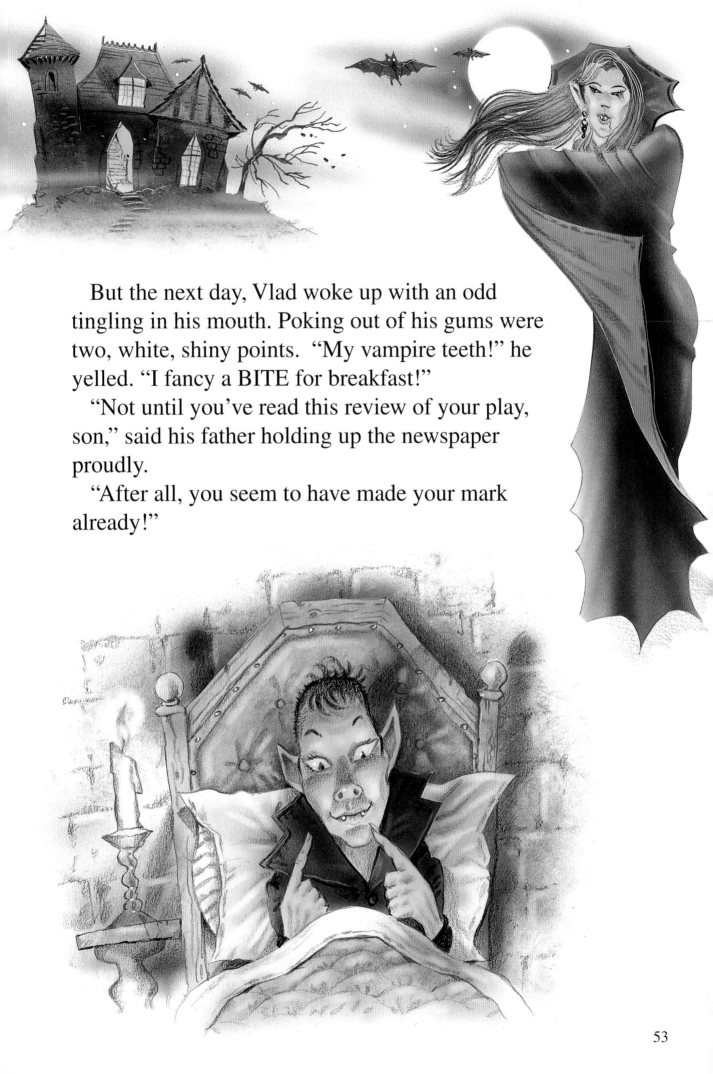

But the next day, Vlad woke up with an odd tingling in his mouth. Poking out of his gums were two, white, shiny points. "My vampire teeth!" he yelled. "I fancy a BITE for breakfast!"

"Not until you've read this review of your play, son," said his father holding up the newspaper proudly.

"After all, you seem to have made your mark already!"

Ode to Ghosts

A ghost he has a sad old life
Haunting empty castles.
On birthdays and at Christmastime
The mailman brings no parcels.

He floats around from room to room,
He howls and clanks his chains.
But everyone ignores the noise,
And blames it on the drains.

And if by chance he should appear
Most people scream with fright.
He just can't understand it—
Is he such a dreadful sight?

He has no friends to play with
It really is a shame.
He'd like to come around for tea,
Or join you in a game.

But people think that ghosts are bad
And so they stay away.
There's no one he can chatter to,
Or pass the time of day.

So if you ever meet a ghost
Don't run away in fright.
Stay awhile and have a chat,
You'll find they're most polite.

Peg's Pepper

Peg the witch lived with her black cat, Pepper, in a crooked cottage, deep in a wood. She spent her time making bubbling brews and spectacular spells, which didn't always work. Elves and fairies would ask her to cure anything from a sore tooth to a broken wing. So Peg's time passed busily enough.

She was never lonely either, not with Pepper purring about the place. He followed her everywhere. If the witch was in her yard, gathering herbs or other more unpleasant ingredients for the cauldron, Pepper would stalk her through the long grass then pop out playfully. If Peg was sitting by the fire, studying her spell book, Pepper would curl up contentedly on her lap.

Even when Peg took night flights on her broomstick, Pepper tagged along. He would sink his sharp claws into the handle to get a good grip. Then Peg and Pepper would whizz away up past the moon.

The truth was, Peg and Pepper were perfect company for each other. That is, until something strange happened.

"A...atchooo!" Peg suddenly sneezed as she sat gently brushing Pepper's dark fur, which

shone like polished coal. The witch's long
nose began to itch and twitch and her eyes
started to water.

"Don't tell me I've caught a cold,"
she said, crossly. "I shouldn't have stayed out
so late last night, in the cold, chasing shooting
stars on my broomstick. A...ATCHOOOO!"

This time, Peg sneezed so hard her pointed
hat slipped over her eyes. Pepper meowed
sympathetically while the witch went to get a
handkerchief from the washing line.

Outside in the fresh air, she stopped
sneezing straight away. But Pepper followed
her out and brushed against her, hoping to
be stroked. No sooner had Peg bent down to
stroke him, than she sneezed again; not once,
not twice, but three times!

Back indoors, it was even worse. Whenever
Pepper came too close, Peg started sneezing.

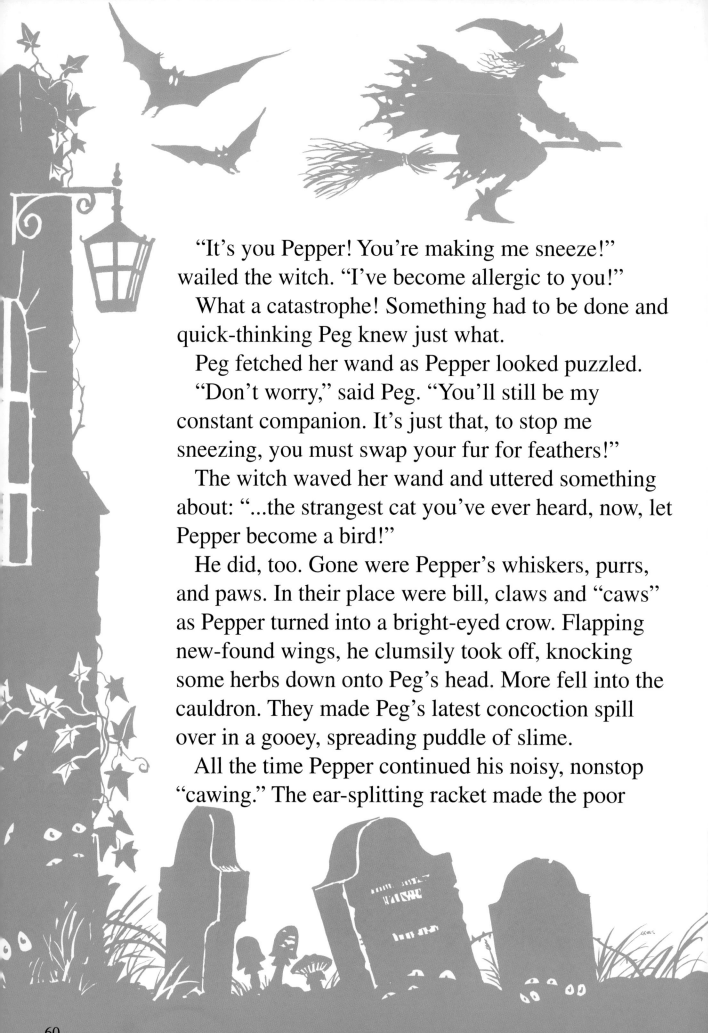

"It's you Pepper! You're making me sneeze!" wailed the witch. "I've become allergic to you!"

What a catastrophe! Something had to be done and quick-thinking Peg knew just what.

Peg fetched her wand as Pepper looked puzzled.

"Don't worry," said Peg. "You'll still be my constant companion. It's just that, to stop me sneezing, you must swap your fur for feathers!"

The witch waved her wand and uttered something about: "...the strangest cat you've ever heard, now, let Pepper become a bird!"

He did, too. Gone were Pepper's whiskers, purrs, and paws. In their place were bill, claws and "caws" as Pepper turned into a bright-eyed crow. Flapping new-found wings, he clumsily took off, knocking some herbs down onto Peg's head. More fell into the cauldron. They made Peg's latest concoction spill over in a gooey, spreading puddle of slime.

All the time Pepper continued his noisy, nonstop "cawing." The ear-splitting racket made the poor

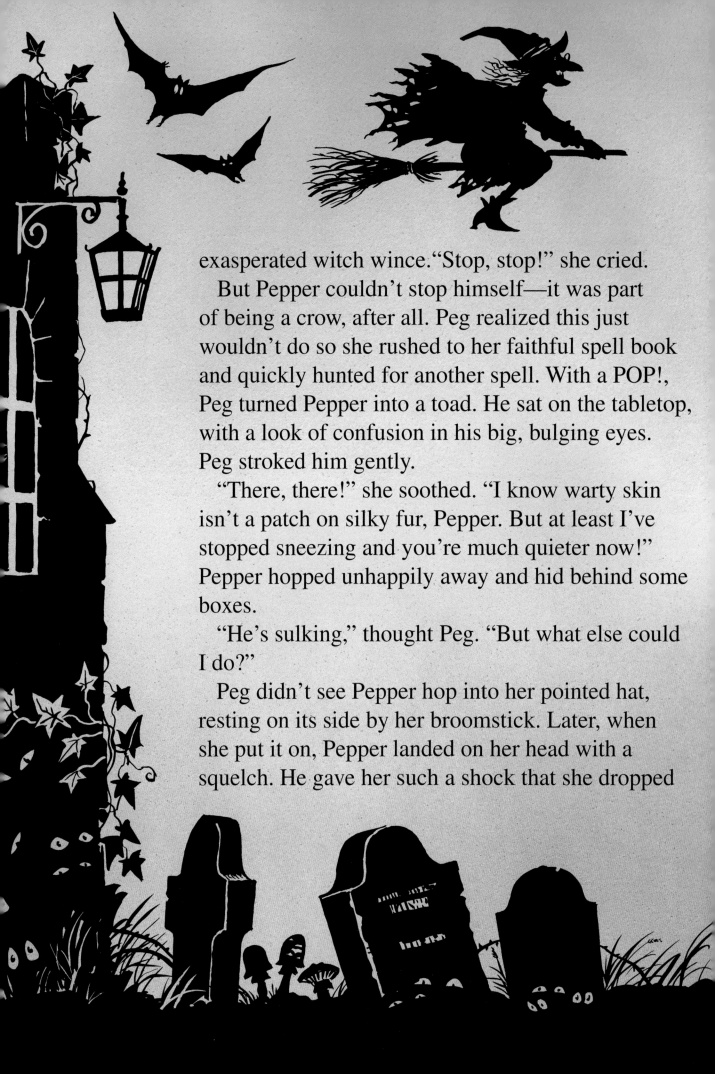

exasperated witch wince. "Stop, stop!" she cried.

But Pepper couldn't stop himself—it was part of being a crow, after all. Peg realized this just wouldn't do so she rushed to her faithful spell book and quickly hunted for another spell. With a POP!, Peg turned Pepper into a toad. He sat on the tabletop, with a look of confusion in his big, bulging eyes. Peg stroked him gently.

"There, there!" she soothed. "I know warty skin isn't a patch on silky fur, Pepper. But at least I've stopped sneezing and you're much quieter now!" Pepper hopped unhappily away and hid behind some boxes.

"He's sulking," thought Peg. "But what else could I do?"

Peg didn't see Pepper hop into her pointed hat, resting on its side by her broomstick. Later, when she put it on, Pepper landed on her head with a squelch. He gave her such a shock that she dropped

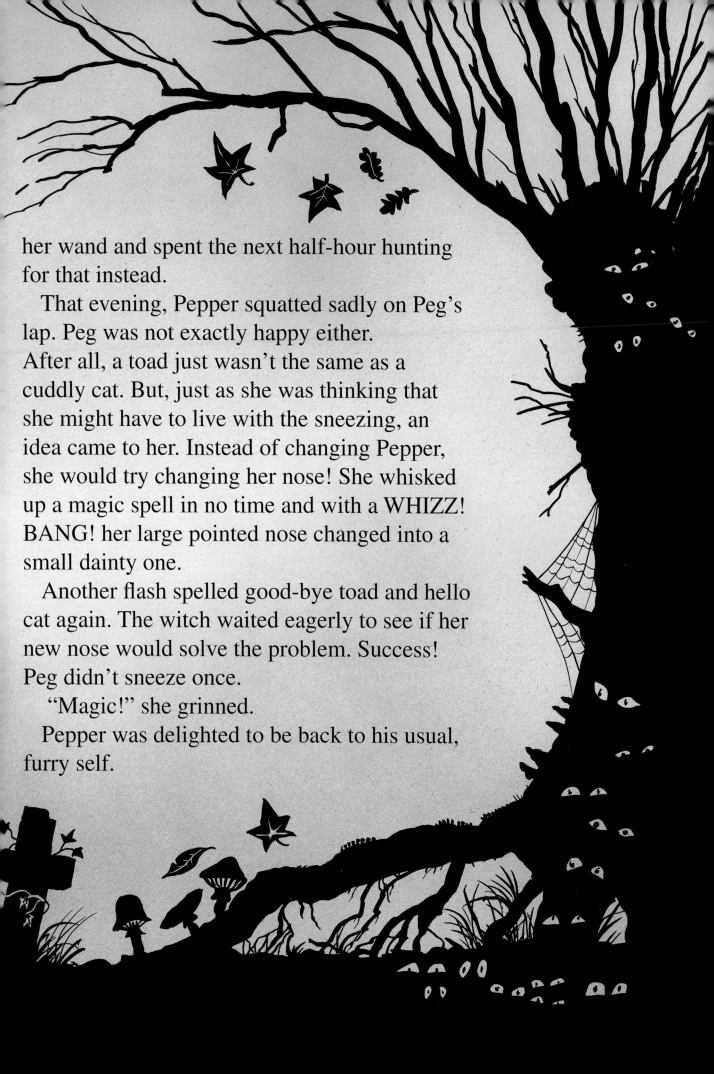

her wand and spent the next half-hour hunting
for that instead.

That evening, Pepper squatted sadly on Peg's
lap. Peg was not exactly happy either.
After all, a toad just wasn't the same as a
cuddly cat. But, just as she was thinking that
she might have to live with the sneezing, an
idea came to her. Instead of changing Pepper,
she would try changing her nose! She whisked
up a magic spell in no time and with a WHIZZ!
BANG! her large pointed nose changed into a
small dainty one.

Another flash spelled good-bye toad and hello
cat again. The witch waited eagerly to see if her
new nose would solve the problem. Success!
Peg didn't sneeze once.

"Magic!" she grinned.

Pepper was delighted to be back to his usual,
furry self.

"Not even a tickle from my new, little nose!" cackled Peg, picking up Pepper and stroking him. "I'm cured!"

Pepper purred loudly. But Peg suddenly stopped laughing and uttered a faint sound.

"Hic!"

At the same time, Pepper felt Peg's shoulders shake. It only lasted a second. But then it happened again, and again.

"Hic! Hic!" The sound only stopped when Peg put Pepper down.

"Great slithering slugs!" shrieked the witch. "My spell's misfired! Now see what you make me do, Pepper! "

But Pepper didn't wait to see anything! He'd had enough changing shape for one day. The last thing he wanted was to be

turned into a rat, hedgehog, or anything else Peg may care to think of. Pepper hurtled outside while Peg rushed for her spell book. Thumbing through her spell book for Magic Cures, she looked up the letter "H."

"'Hairy hands, horrible howls'," she read, urgently. "I know it's here somewhere. How do you spell hiccups?!"

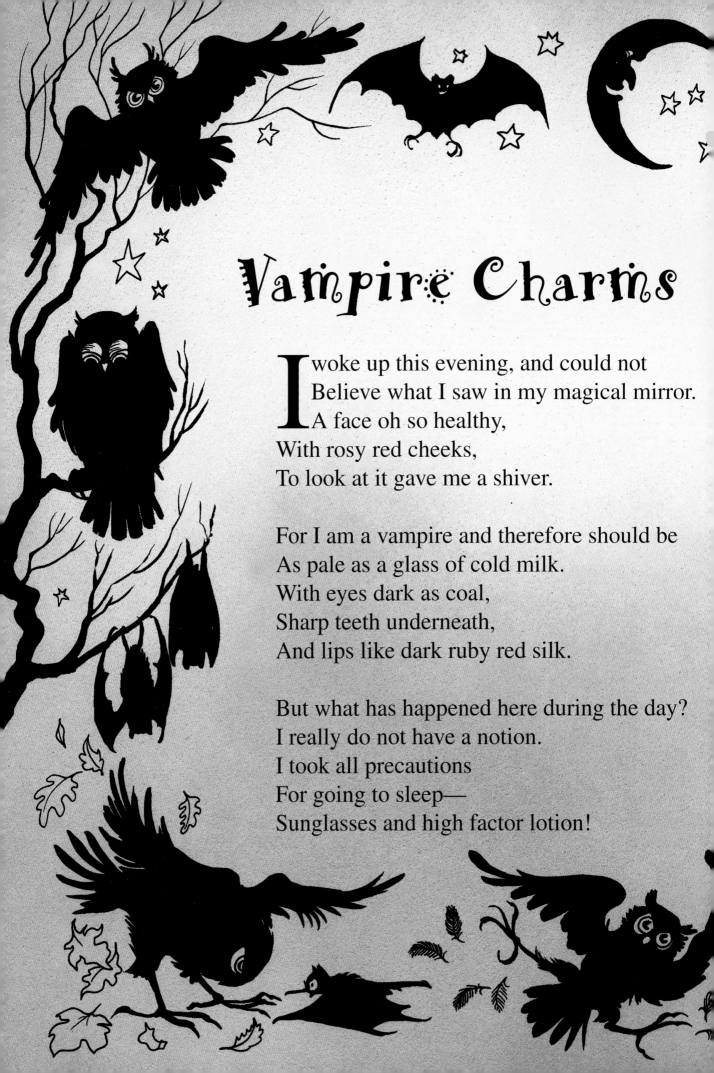

Vampire Charms

I woke up this evening, and could not
Believe what I saw in my magical mirror.
A face oh so healthy,
With rosy red cheeks,
To look at it gave me a shiver.

For I am a vampire and therefore should be
As pale as a glass of cold milk.
With eyes dark as coal,
Sharp teeth underneath,
And lips like dark ruby red silk.

But what has happened here during the day?
I really do not have a notion.
I took all precautions
For going to sleep—
Sunglasses and high factor lotion!

But somehow the sun has crept into the room,
And entered a chink in my coffin.
To guess what the others
Will say when they see,
You don't have to be a real boffin!

For they'll laugh and gossip, point fingers and say
"Oh the sunkissed look must be in fashion!
She thinks that a sun tan
Will increase her charm,
When we all know vampires should look ashen!"

So I think I'll stay put in my coffin for now,
At least until this deep tan has faded.
I just hope in a while I'll be looking unfit,
And with luck just a little bit jaded!

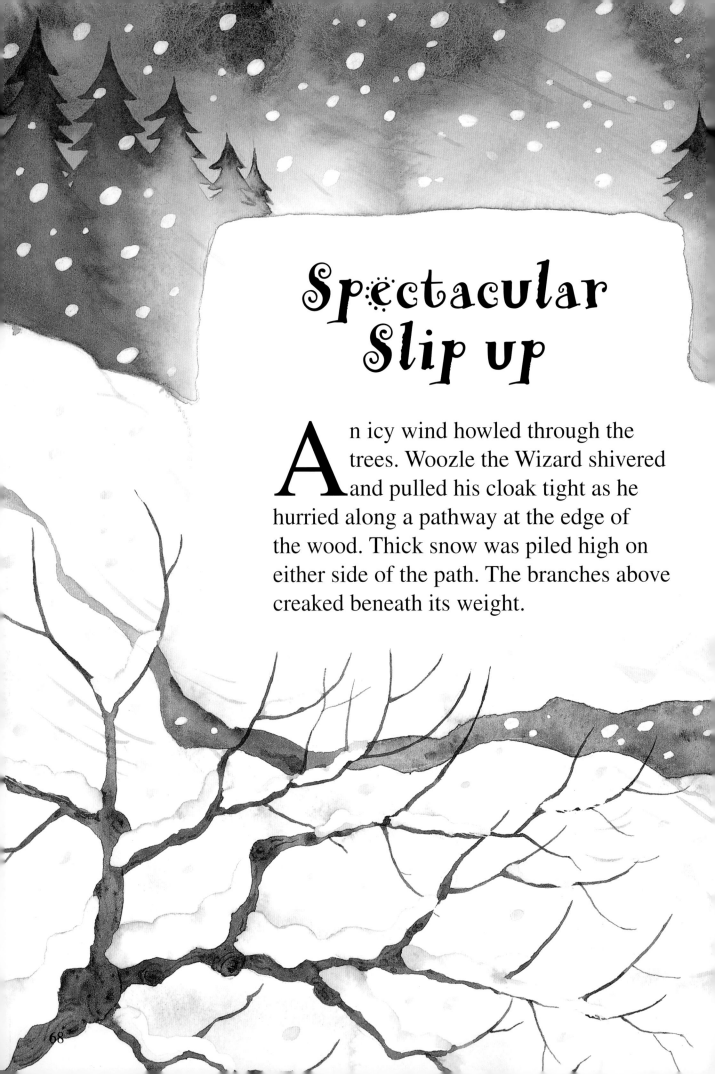

Spectacular Slip up

An icy wind howled through the trees. Woozle the Wizard shivered and pulled his cloak tight as he hurried along a pathway at the edge of the wood. Thick snow was piled high on either side of the path. The branches above creaked beneath its weight.

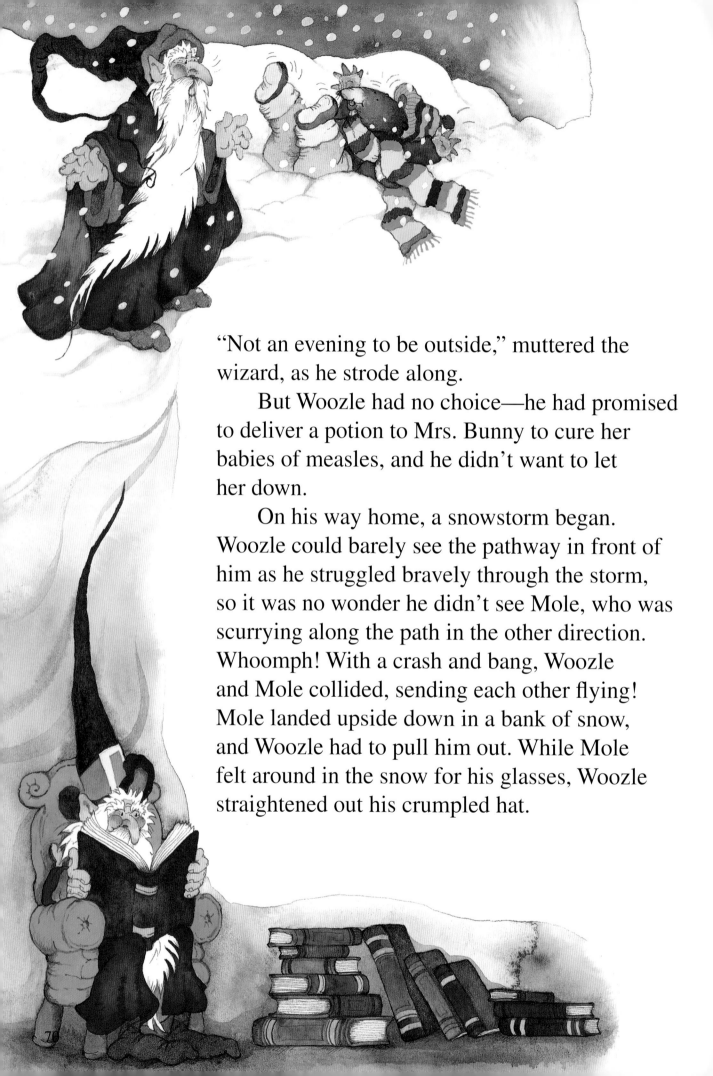

"Not an evening to be outside," muttered the wizard, as he strode along.

But Woozle had no choice—he had promised to deliver a potion to Mrs. Bunny to cure her babies of measles, and he didn't want to let her down.

On his way home, a snowstorm began. Woozle could barely see the pathway in front of him as he struggled bravely through the storm, so it was no wonder he didn't see Mole, who was scurrying along the path in the other direction. Whoomph! With a crash and bang, Woozle and Mole collided, sending each other flying! Mole landed upside down in a bank of snow, and Woozle had to pull him out. While Mole felt around in the snow for his glasses, Woozle straightened out his crumpled hat.

Then, after checking that no one was hurt, they each continued on their way.

Back at home, Woozle settled down for a nice evening of "spelling." He took down his spell book and felt in his pocket for his reading glasses, but they weren't there. "Now what have I done with them?" he muttered to himself crossly. He looked around but they were nowhere to be found. "Oh, well, I shall just have to manage without," he said, turning the pages of his spell book. "Here we are—Frog into Teapot. I could use a new teapot!"

Peering closely at the recipe, he gathered the ingredients and mixed up a magic potion in his cauldron. Then, taking a nice fat frog down from the shelf, he sprinkled it with the potion, and waved his magic wand.

"Make me a shiny little teapot," cried the wizard. With a whoosh, the frog disappeared and in its place stood a tiny metal robot.

"Oh, dear," said Woozle. "I must have misread something. Still, a robot could be useful," he said.

Woozle tried another spell—Slug into Bowl of Fruit. But this time when he waved his wand a rubber boot appeared. "That's no use at all," sighed Woozle.

He tried to turn a snail into hot toast, but instead he got a fat ghost, and in place of a chocolate cake he got a garden rake.

"I give up," Woozle sighed. He sat back in his armchair and closed his eyes to think. Where had he put his glasses?

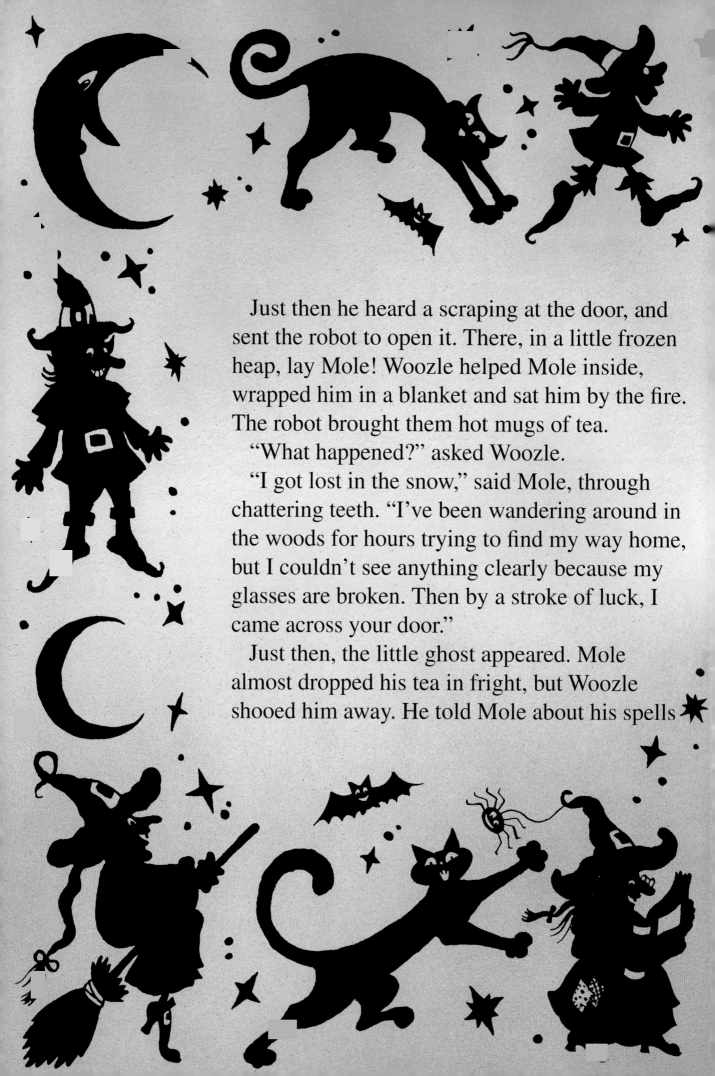

Just then he heard a scraping at the door, and sent the robot to open it. There, in a little frozen heap, lay Mole! Woozle helped Mole inside, wrapped him in a blanket and sat him by the fire. The robot brought them hot mugs of tea.

"What happened?" asked Woozle.

"I got lost in the snow," said Mole, through chattering teeth. "I've been wandering around in the woods for hours trying to find my way home, but I couldn't see anything clearly because my glasses are broken. Then by a stroke of luck, I came across your door."

Just then, the little ghost appeared. Mole almost dropped his tea in fright, but Woozle shooed him away. He told Mole about his spells

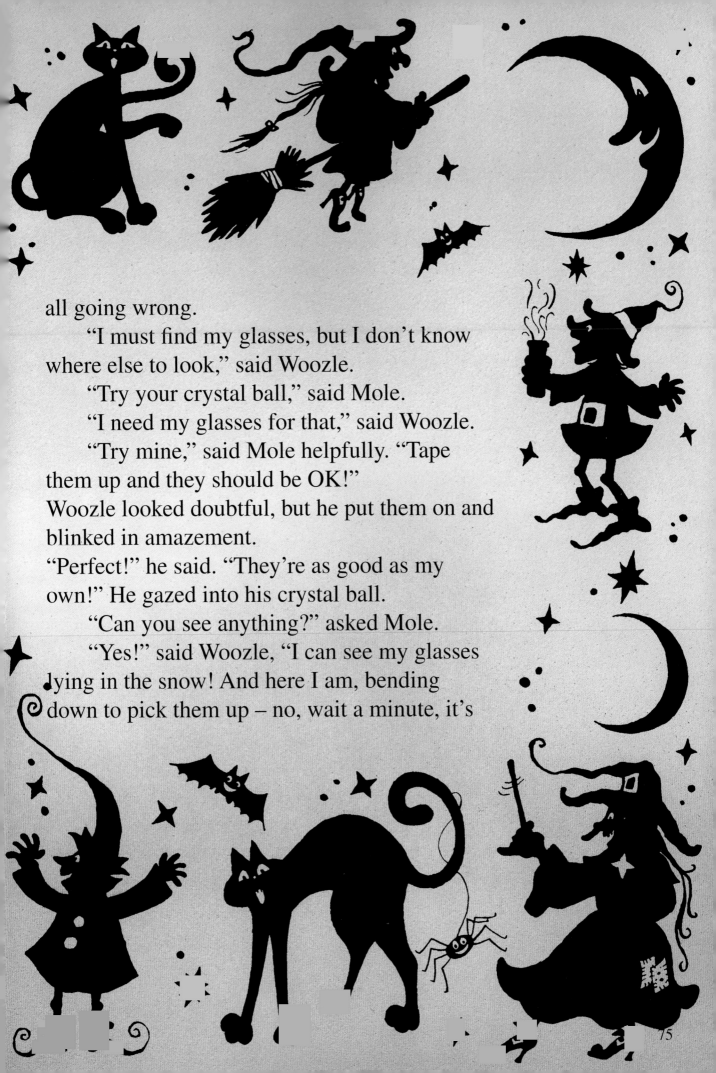

all going wrong.

"I must find my glasses, but I don't know where else to look," said Woozle.

"Try your crystal ball," said Mole.

"I need my glasses for that," said Woozle.

"Try mine," said Mole helpfully. "Tape them up and they should be OK!"
Woozle looked doubtful, but he put them on and blinked in amazement.
"Perfect!" he said. "They're as good as my own!" He gazed into his crystal ball.

"Can you see anything?" asked Mole.

"Yes!" said Woozle, "I can see my glasses lying in the snow! And here I am, bending down to pick them up – no, wait a minute, it's

not me, it's you! You're putting the glasses in
your pocket!"

"But how can they be mine, when mine are
here?" asked Mole, puzzled.
Woozle scratched his head, thinking hard.

"I've got it! My glasses must have fallen out
of my pocket when we bumped into each other,
and you must have picked them up by mistake.
Which means that your glasses are still in the
snow, and my glasses are, well—they're right
here on the end of my nose where they belong!"
The two friends chuckled at the
mix-up!

In no time, Woozle, using his own glasses to
read the spells carefully this time, changed the
rubber boot into a bowl of fruit, and the rake

into chocolate cake, just as he had wanted all
along. So, the friends tucked into a delicious
tea, served up by the robot, who Woozle
decided was more use than a teapot by far,
and entertained by the ghost, who was very
good at telling spooky stories.

Maybe the long, cold winter would pass
quite pleasantly after all!